This Little Tiger book belongs to:

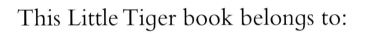

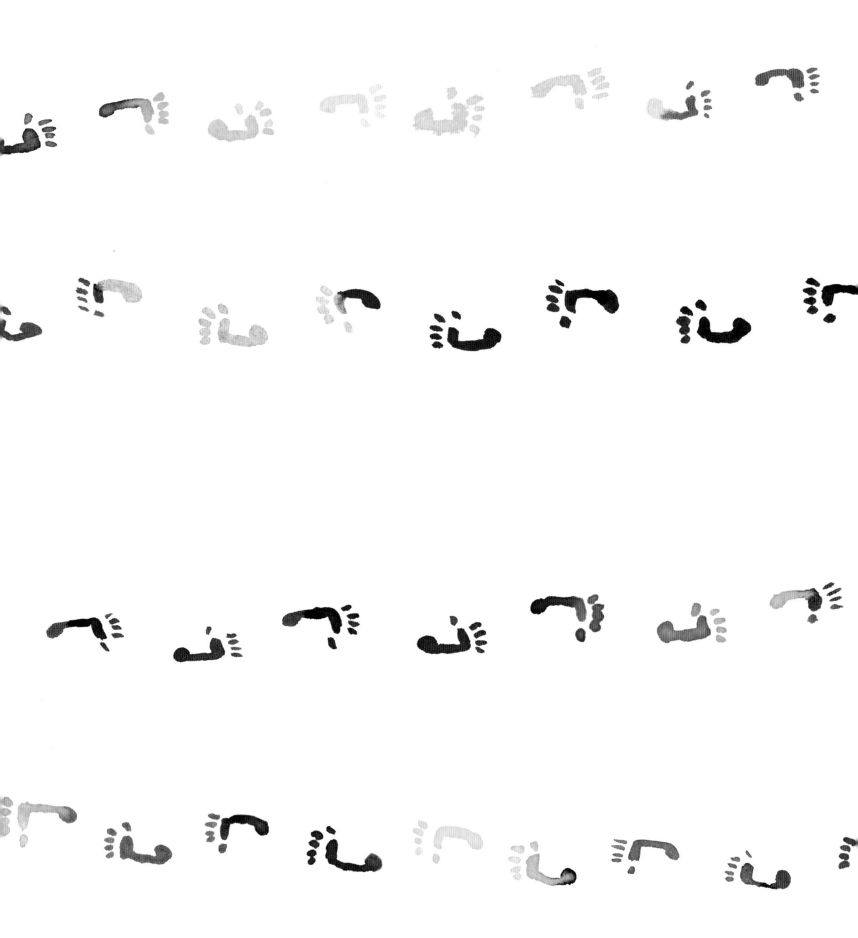

To Ben, who painted Tucker pink
*when **he** was a little monkey*
~ S S

To Mary
~ N S

LITTLE TIGER
An imprint of Little Tiger Press Limited
1 Coda Studios, 189 Munster Road, London SW6 6AW
Imported into the EEA by Penguin Random House Ireland,
Morrison Chambers, 32 Nassau Street, Dublin D02 YH68
www.littletiger.co.uk

First published in Great Britain 2007
This edition published 2020

A CIP catalogue record for this book is available
from the British Library

Printed in China • LTP/2700/5100/0423

10 9 8 7

The Monkey with a Bright Blue Bottom

Steve Smallman

Nick Schon

LITTLE TiGER

LONDON

A long time ago, when the world was quite new,
a monkey sat watching the birds as they flew.
Like feathery rainbows they flashed through the air.
"How come they're so pretty?" he thought. "It's not fair!"

All round him were creatures of every sort,
some fat and some skinny,
    some tall and some short,
But none of them purple or yellow or blue;
they all looked as dull as an elephant poo.

The monkey walked down to the stream with a sigh,
then a vivid blue kingfisher bird darted by.
He followed it down to a gap in the rushes
and there was a paintbox with one or two brushes.

He snatched up the paintbox as quick as a wink,
tried painting some flowers and then had a think:
"Somebody painted this kingfisher blue,
I'm going to paint all the animals too!"

The animals always get out of the sun
and go for a nap at a quarter to one.
So when he was sure everybody was sleeping,
with paintbox and brushes the monkey came creeping.

He painted some frogs and a couple of snakes
and thought to himself, "What a difference it makes!"
Then feeling much bolder, the cheeky young fellow
set to and painted a leopard bright yellow.

Just then the big cat gave a growl in his sleep
and monkey shot into a tree with a leap.
The black paint dropped out with a splash from the box,
and fell on the leopard in little black spots.

"That's great!" said the monkey,
 then, just for a laugh,
he painted brown squares on a yellow giraffe,
Black stripes on a zebra and white on a skunk,
and both on the lemur asleep in his bunk.

"Hee hee!" laughed the monkey. "I'm having such fun!"
then he spotted a bear fast asleep in the sun.
He took out his brush and then, what a surprise,
he painted white spectacles round the bear's eyes!

Bear woke with a start and yelled,
  "WHAT DID YOU DO?"
Which woke up the rest of the animals too.
The monkey was so scared he practically fainted,
surrounded by all of the creatures he'd painted.

They all started yelling till bear shouted, "HUSH!"
Then quietly picked up the paintbox and brush.
He painted the monkey's face red, white and blue.
and then for good luck did his bottom end too!

And still to this day when the monkey goes by,
the animals giggle, they laugh till they cry.
His bum is still blue as a bright summer sky,
he looks like a clown – and now you know why!

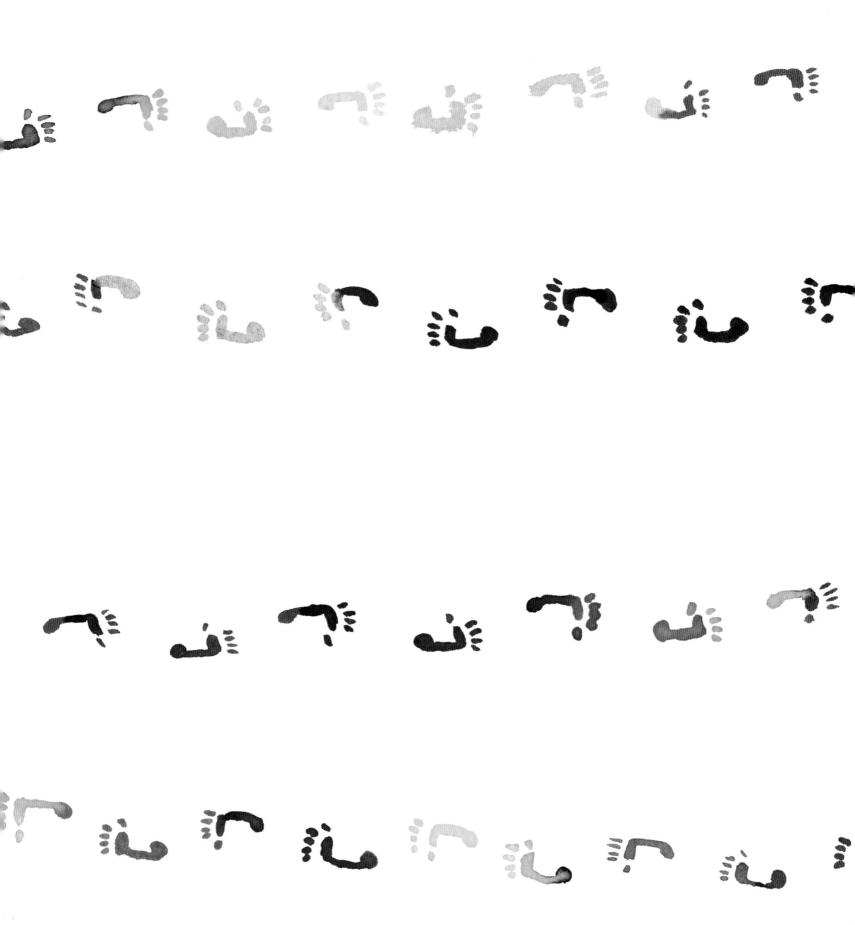